SUMEET KUMAR , A adult who experinces many phases of life , a well known writer and a writer of new era .In reality he is a writer as well as ,singer ,poeter ,shayar ,quote writer ,lyric writer and and a performer well as anchor or standup comedian.Very exicting and intresting fact about him is that he is author of new era i.e.

He starts his journey of writing at the age when he was going to schools to get the study .

His streak of 200 books will be the great achievment for him in future ,His some famous works i.e Maturity of love (genre _Love) Privacy of dream (Genre -LIFE STYLE OF MIDDLE CLASS).

you can also buy his book from NOTION PRESS ,ABE BOOKS ,IMUSIC IN ,FLIPKART ,AMAZON ,KINDLE ,INSTANT READ LIKE EBOOK ,KINDLE ,GOOGLE ,INTERNATIONAL SITES AND MANY MORE .

PODCASTER ON SPOTIFY :@BROKEN HEART

INSTA ID : BOOKHUB92

GMAIL: sumitkumar 88234

LINKEDIAN : SUMEET KUMAR

.

Contents

Contents

MISSION SAFFRON

THE LAST MARTYR

SUMEET KUMAR

Made with ♥ on the Notion Press Platform
www.notionpress.com

Preface

The pain is borne by the one who knows how long its pain is going to be even after that, he teaches everyone through his education that even if it comes to the point of death, do not allow your country to become a slave again. And don't know about whom I am talking about my army brothers.

Being in the military means heaven.

Acknowledgements

SUMEET KUMAR , A adult who experinces many phases of life , a well known writer and a writer of new era .In reality he is a writer as well as ,singer ,poeter ,shayar ,quote writer ,lyric writer and and a performer well as anchor or standup comedian.Very exicting and intresting fact about him is that he is author of new era i.e.

He starts his journey of writing at the age when he was going to schools to get the study .

His streak of 200 books will be the great achievment for him in future ,His some famous works i.e Maturity of love (genre _Love) Privacy of dream (Genre -LIFE STYLE OF MIDDLE CLASS).

you can also buy his book from NOTION PRESS ,ABE BOOKS ,IMUSIC IN ,FLIPKART ,AMAZON ,KINDLE ,INSTANT READ LIKE EBOOK ,KINDLE ,GOOGLE ,INTERNATIONAL SITES AND MANY MORE .

PODCASTER ON SPOTIFY :@BROKEN HEART

INSTA ID : BOOKHUB92

GMAIL: sumitkumar 88234

LINKEDIAN : SUMEET KUMAR

.

CHAPTER ONE

MAGNETISM OF KINDNESS

Whatever I am writing today, every narration of it is very different from me, even after six months, I cannot share my condition and feelings in front of anyone, because neither the public is worthy of me nor I am worthy of them, yet with time Neither I can stay away from him nor he can stay away from me, I have not been able to understand life till date that what is wrong with me, because when it comes to dreams, it is different from me, and I don't know when I am going to leave this world, and I don't even know when this world will leave me, why do we feel like we are one? Our life is attached to us, our feelings are attached to us, I and my soul know their specialty, I cannot express a few words of blessings about someone because I know that even if you don't get alms empty handed, then you love someone.

what is will request, well I want to live the journey of God.

Even if life is only of two moments, it is said that if you are very close, then you can never see him in trouble, nor can you ask about him, nor can you celebrate him, still there are some promises. Those who give long to that boundary too and make a new beginning of themselves by being free, I myself do not know my story, means all of you are also thinking that who does not know their own story?

With you even in the words of God, this God wants to stay on your side even in the dead but there is some exhibition which goes through these words to the door which only I can see and no one else, I do not know whether my What's the Story?

CHAPTER TWO

THE BRAVE KING

I don't even know what my life is? But I know about myself what I am and what I have become, neither I have come here to explain my pain nor I am the one who starts something that hurts me, this is neither Heer Ranjhe's Nor is anyone Romeo.

This story of Juliet is of that witness, who has lost his Even lost his life, people say that if you are a human being, you will love only a human being or not, God is a permanent creature on earth, so why should you love only a human being? This is also a question, why shouldn't I love the air whose winds keep me alive even today, why shouldn't I love the sunlight seeing which I start each new day.

It is not necessary to love that attraction is needed, if your condition matches then it is not called love, it is called compromise and if your life matches then it is not called love, it is called trust, well I said earlier also that this is not a story. some is based on love and not on living and dying, leaving aside its words, we go on a journey from where the world seems different.

It was only a few days back when I met an eyewitness like things did not match with his face, I thought let's get to know eyewitness, because when you don't see anything in your life then at the same time The life of the society has nothing to do with you, it is just giving you time to understand yourself, and when I witnessed that .

CHAPTER THREE

GOD IS PERMANENT

The one who lost his life to get himself, people say that if you are a human being then you will love only a human being or else, God is a permanent creature on earth, so why should you love only a human being? This is also a question, why shouldn't I love that wind whose winds keep me alive even today, why shouldn't I love that sunlight seeing which I start each new day, love It is not necessary to have attraction, if you meet then it is not called love, it is called compromise and if you meet your life then it is called love, not trust, well I had said earlier also that this story is neither a story nor a kiss. It is not based on love nor on living and dying, leaving its words, we go on a journey where The world seems a bit different.

It was only a few days back when I mct an cycwitness like things did not match with his face, I thought let's get to know eyewitness, because when you don't see anything in your life then at the same time The life of the society has nothing to do with you, it is just giving you time to understand yourself, and when I witnessed that

When I listened to things, I also felt that maybe people seem to be crazy about gatherings, when I asked if you have any problem, he told me that the problem is life whose sun is fixed on my life and death, first of all his words sometimes seemed confusing to me, because at that time there was no society in him that this witness

What does he want to say to me, I asked him again and again that do you have any problem, even then he repeated the same words which he had spoken earlier, I do not know what he wanted to say to me?

CHAPTER FOUR

PURPORT OF MIRROR

But for some time, but I tried to understand him, I followed him in love too, and when he was crushed, his memories were like him, his broken homes and every happiness, at that time I was feeling as if life wanted to tell me something else and maybe did not want to understand even after understanding it.

When you are in dire need of someone, then you cannot live without his memories, you will kill a lot at that time, you will leave so much that in any way he is with you and does not go anywhere, but is he really close to you? It is because of this fear that he has come close to you, I have seen the relationships of today which are very different from your thinking, you The closer you go to him, the more he will distance you from himself. When I fell in love for the first time, my feelings were very different. For that one person, I started understanding everything in him, but it is said that when she breaks down, it is because of her noise. Everything also goes, neither the same thing remains in it after it is broken nor its nature is good at that time.

Will be able to understand from it, nor is it clearly visible to any face like a mirror.

CHAPTER FIVE

ACCEPTANCE THE SORROW

Man talks a lot about time that let the time come, you will be punished for your deeds, let this time come, you will get the fruits of your deeds, don't know about the fruits, but there is a lot of sorrow in life and you have got so many that you still see So my eyes fill with tears and my tears dry up, yet I wait for this day to pass and the next day begins.

But it has not happened till date, neither that day has come nor it has started, yet the wait is still there, a man's life does not have that much hopebut they brings happiness to his family and being a joker himself makes the whole world laugh, and I have seen people like this too.

Whose every desire runs only in the name of love, and nothing more can be done because frogs may give you peace but love gives life and this life is very important for someone.

When I cried for the first time, I was the one to wipe my own tears and I was also the one to talk about my own sorrows, but it is not necessary that you stay with yourself all the time, this life looks like a dream that we never Can't even complete, I can say that moments can't express in front of everyone what I have felt myself, I feel that I am why those Among people who only need me, not love me, why did I get into such a relationship with them whose importance is also like that moon which is visible every night but it has no existence without the light of that sun, right? Only he has any charity, in the same way we humans are also meant for meaning, my training to say is that people remember you only then.

Do it when your need is very much missed by them, even my time is not enough for anyone to understand what is my need?

CHAPTER SIX

SUPPORT OF BIRTH

Since birth, every story of mine is built on the same thing, whose identity is so much that we are what? Means what is the need of a human being, I am not talking about science nor I am talking about attached progress, because as far as I can think, I have seen that many years when mankind has created When he was born, he was human at that time.

Love was not even known to the public, nor did they feel it, yet their life went ahead and they became more and more successful in their lives, till date I have not been able to understand how this thing called love came into life. Neither their thinking has been determined in the texts nor its environment has been decided by humans , when humans connected with each other.

If we are connected, then what is the environment of his feelings, what is love, the relationships we make, is it a test of love, if it is love that people consider sacred, then why hasn't it been surrounded, we have created it, and we have A new world has been created, but this world is also given to them, the story of our birth is not new, it is old, in the sense of saying ,

I want her upbringing is so simple that the death of the human race has never happened, our death has never been fixed, when a human dies, at that time we only burn her sari, not her soul, the soul So she remains free even when her body is burnt,I want to say that the story of a human can be immortal, because he himself is immortal, even though his sarees are burnt, but his death does not happen in reality, we never die, there are some steps of long time which Walks two steps ahead of us.

CHAPTER SEVEN

SPARK OF PAIN

I don't understand my own life, how will we understand any love, that Krishna is also far away without his Radha, he also had a love story but both of them never got married, every little one of them was killed today.

God remembers the world, but our love is like a burning fire whose spark ignites his laptop for some timeI don't understand my own life, how will we understand any love, that Krishna is also far away without his Radha, he also had a love story but both of them never got married, every little one of them was killed today. God remembers the world, but our love is like a burning fire whose spark ignites his laptop for some time

So there is Aarti, but after a while, every identity of her gets erased, like that ash, like every habit of recognizing is the evening of darkness, I am not saying that do not remove your pain which is in your part, I am Saying this, try to understand the pain in your part because no one's identity remains incomplete, the life of a human being, his many meanings if we understand from the same way, I don't need any penance to remove my own pain and sorrow with it, I just need to recognize what has been lost due to relationships and in that fog I can't find Ara, I don't know how far he is from me, I just know that he is not in my part now, but there is no such thing that I will not search for him, I will surely do because this world is mine except him. is also incomplete.

some story is not called immortal just like that, in reality those people are already immortal because their story is also called immortal .

CHAPTER EIGHT

SOIL AS MOTHER

Life always sees many faces in which some are unknown and some are our own, but what is the welfare of all, we all know that the nature of a person does not change by changing the face, yet love is such a fire that every person It destroys only by taking it close to you, no matter how far you are, this story is neither of Majnu nor this is the story of Laila, the immortal young man who surrendered his life to the country in his childhood, which he used to consider as his home, a person can be separated from his saree for some time but never from his soul No, I don't know why I am writing his story, neither the story is related to his love nor his identity, The story is written from his immortal story, which everyone knows, they say that our military brothers are just like the sun, whose light keeps the whole world away from darkness, they don't just protect us, they help us in every way. Days take us towards a new life, without them this life is just like a stone which has no desire.

Yes, I never thought that I would try to write such a story in my own words, but today I write feeling proud of myself, I do not know whether I will ever meet him, yet I know that much if she is not in our life, then in our life too she is like a flower which withers when it gets sunlight on time.

It goes, it vanishes itself in the well of the grave, what can I say about our country, this India is not just our pride but our life, and we can do anything for it, where people in other countries Soil is called soil, in India we call her as mother, many things are unknown about which we know every day till date.

CHAPTER NINE

COUNTRY LOVE

Take the love of our country just like the moon which protects us from the blind and also makes us realize that we are not alone in this world where man brings his wealth for himself to save himself. It is our soldiers who fight, who take their lives for their country, we cannot say humans at all, even if a person sacrifices his life for others Since when did you start giving, our military brother is not human at all, he is like that God who does not stay with us well but always helps us and protects us. Before telling anything, there are some words that I want to say and everything is like that .

CHAPTER TEN

DEMAND OF POSITION

"ONLY A
SOLDIER
CAN UNDERSTAND
THE
LIFE
OF A
SOLDIER."

CHAPTER ELEVEN

BORN FOR FIGHT

RANVEER SHEKHAWAT

MAJOR SQUAD 52 A

POSTING : KARACHI (Pakistan)

It is clear from the name that this story is not of a human being, it is a soldier, of a soldier who sacrificed his life to save his country, on the same day he had to wear the uniform, this is a common story. Like the rest, it can be said that this is a story of a great witness, because our military brothers are the protectors of the land and because of their love for their mother India, they are always attached to their land, post them anywhere in the world. even then Flags also come from home only, this is the lion of our India whose story of jungle is not famous, but how he hunts is famous, there is no one bigger than him in the world, if there is anyone below that one then he is , Why am I saying such a thing, even this will raise curtains because this story is in the name of his brave soldiers, well now my journey ends because the story of our chief Ranveer Shekhawat is about to begin.

CHAPTER TWELVE

SAVE THE SOIL MOTHER

Karachi, like the city, it is also its abuses, earlier it was also ours, but we donated it to our neighbour , thinking that they might die of hunger, that there is no special hatred for the community, Because that too before itself, but that government's talk is different because it is a lot of work to think, but it seems to be different , like that, only I know about this operation and no one else, not even left companions, we soldiers. What is it, send it anywhere, we have to kill and save our country.

In that gift, the same path of victory has to be climbed, however, the life of us soldiers is very special, because we carry the shroud with us every day. It is not a matter of luxury that we do not have the luxury of living, these are not our dreams, they are and our dreams are that we can do anything for the pride of our soil, if even a small drop from the other side is ours. If they scratches our soil mother, we will kill them by entering because it is not just our soil, it is our mother.

I had never thought since childhood that I would ever join the army, it does not mean that I did not have this desire, I did not want to become one, but it is said that if the defense of the country is not handed over to the right hands, then life will end. We pride ourselves on being part of the country.

Because we don't choose that uniform, that uniform chooses us, even in love I think I will not put it on my saree until I become capable of it, this is my respect, and my desire too, wrapped in this The pride of the country is divided and in love they even sacrifice themselves for the country, it is not just a uniform but a passion.

CHAPTER THIRTEEN

ARJUN SHEKHAWAT

When I was 15 years old dad says that if you walk with the country, the country will also walk with you. If you want some wealth, then earn the affection of that mother, who even after hiding her anger, sent her only son to that war. There is no hope of returning from the war, yet she sends her son because even if he is killed in that war

She will accept her victory, because he is not fighting this war only for himself, he is fighting for her mother India, whose many sons protect their country and their mother earth even after losing their lives.

We Indians are sentimental that too a lot because we run our country with our heart and not with our mind, the feeling of love is alive everywhere, If love is alive in this world because this is India,

Well if I start these lamps of words then my story was incomplete maybe ?

Life was very good till 18, means hanging out with friends, then studying and playing this was life, that had thought but never thought that years are increasing but age is also bad with it, and with age the dreams of father are also increasing, Arjun Shekhawat, my father is also the life of the country But he never told me what it was, neither mother knew about his work nor he used to tell Kishi about his work, everyone thought the same.

CHAPTER FOURTEEN

THE MARTYR OF TRICOLOR

I used to think that he is a teacher, but he was not completely true, seeing dad never felt that he is a teacher, if asked me, I asked dad many times if you are really a teacher. ? And after that dad used to tell me all the time that you love your father, and I used to tell him at that time too that no dad, I trust you, That little nudge of his used to be our whole life, then one day suddenly after almost six months when no story of dad came, we had understood that he is no more in this world, neither I nor he. I do not want to remember that day nor do I want to tell the memories of that day to anyone from here, but even today I can say that I am proud that I

Arjun is the son of Shekhawat, I belong to him, I am the son of that father, I was the first love of my country and later his family, I am not angry with him that he is no longer with us, I am happy that he has done his duty Play it from the right date, when every body of his complete wrapped in that tricolor and then cam to our door , then at that time, there was a voice everywhere that Arjun Shekhawat should remain immortal...

CHAPTER FIFTEEN

THE TEARS OF MIRROR

Tears in my eyes that day, for my dad that respect which I could never give to that dream, Sayyid, after all, what do you do? Means neither do they tell their family members nor do they ever let themselves feel it, they need love, they worry about their country, they die for their soil and they live for their soil When ma saw dad, she became completely silent at that time, seeing her silence, I got scared for some time.

Was, I don't know what to do in that time? How to handle them, I was not feeling myself alive, I had fainted, I was remembering that last talk of dad, I could not accept this thing at that time that my hero is now with me in this world. No, I agree that he was a "hero" for the whole country that day, but for me he was my world.

When I saw ma in that condition, I was very scared, but after some time when Ma went close to Dad and told him that don't worry, your dreams will definitely come true, your Ranveer will also become like you, he one just like you

The son of a soldier will say, and I am proud that I am the wife of Martyr Arjun Shekhwat, seeing my mother, I had decided that day that the one who has handed over her husband to her country, she can never be weak again. It was the anniversary that after my departure, she would go alone, yet she did not retrace her steps, she proudly said in front of everyone that her son would also become a soldier like his father.

CHAPTER SIXTEEN

HERO OF MY LIFE

But I can never be like maybe, she was Jayshe, I will never be like her, I was Jenta, because from childhood I had told dad that I would become a doctor, and dad also promised me that I would I will make you a doctor, I was not able to understand at that time, should I? Can't break Ma's promise because that shroud,

She was attached to the pride of martyr Arjun Shekhawat by placing her hands in front of them, this time could have given up on her dreams, so I thought of becoming a doctor in the army, but they say that the hands of a soldier Until and unless there is a gun mark and the weight of the country is not on the shoulders, he does not become a real soldier, my father single-handedly protected his country by defeating fifty enemies, that too alone, he did not keep his post till his last breath. If I had left, how could I have done this?

CHAPTER SEVENTEEN

SACRIFICE

"SOLDIER MEANS
SACRIFICE
PRIDE
AND
RESPECT
EVEN AFTER
DEATH
WE
REMAIN
ALIVE
FOR
OUR COUNTRY."

CHAPTER EIGHTEEN

ADOPT AS A MAT

I had heard from somewhere that if the path ends, then the destination is almost far away from us, but these things are also incomplete and their reality is also It is incomplete, I never thought that our life would change so much after dad left After leaving, but not good either, Ma was always imprisoned in a silence which neither I could ever take away from her nor she I made a revolution to feel the silence inside myself, I knew that the way our life is entangled I can't confuse myself anymore, the world saw what dad did, but our life was showing us what we couldn't even imagine, money, not every wealth can be bought from, and this thing is known when this dad was not with us, at the age when I was, at that age he himself he could have handled himself, he could have thrown himself in such a fire which was not made for me, Ma did not know how to handle it. life every day I was writing the story of new pain, I did not want sympathy from people that my father is no longer in the world, nor was anyone's love needed, people On the one hand, the truth is shown in films, that after the death of a soldier, his family is respected a lot, respect is given, but it was nothing like that. There was no issue, I could not understand myself, after the departure of dad, everything in his parts was very biting, I If time wants,

I can become like her, I can fulfill my mother's promise, but how can I do it? I didn't know what to do? No line in films matches real life exactly, we see it like this. We see the world as we think and we also see the same Because that thing gives us relief and a lot of peace too, Dad used to say that whatever gives you comfort, you should adopt it as a mat.

CHAPTER NINETEEN

COMFORT IS HELL

If not in my life, she ruined you, and today the same comfort is ruining me, I can't get away from the memories of dad, still with mom The promise has to be fulfilled, after the death of a soldier, not only his family cries, but the whole country cries, and we call that country India. , So I thought that no matter what happens, I will keep my mother's dreams to come true. After about 6 months of dad, I had decided that I will be like him no matter what Just worry about one thing that all the time It was troubling me that if I left then who would stay with ma.

Ma would be left all alone, at that time the thought was something else. Because I had lost my father, but I could not go away from my mother, on the other hand, I could not even break my mother's promise, because the At that time, I had sworn in front of my father, it was not a minor oath, I had thought that day that people knew my father's love, because not today. I have sacrificed my life for my country, but I am not at all like that, I cannot give my life for my country like them, because my mother is alone I can never walk away from the woman who made me proud for nine months and taught me everything in the world that has changed I am today, I cannot make my today, but I will not risk tomorrow, but what about mother's promise? in front of the whole world Said that my son will also become a soldier like his father, it was not that I did not love my country, but I have seen the condition of the world.

CHAPTER TWENTY

THE MARTYR UNIFORM

Nothing else is given, they become immortal for that soil, they ask for that country, but people remember them for some time, then they forget. Let's go, the characters of the film, if you ask anyone, he will tell you in a second, but how many states are there in our India, how many military states are there? comes, and no one will tell how many give their lives for their country.

I had also told my mother at that time that I will not join the army like my father, I do not want to be killed in the eyes of the world for my country. I want to become a doctor, not a soldier, and mother, it is not necessary that if dad does this, I will also do it, I cannot go anywhere leaving you, mother Did not say anything to me at that time but the next day when mother wore dad's uniform and said that even though you love me because I am your mother but Your dad loved his country, isn't his mother, is your dad dead Ranveer, I am proud that my husband has died for the country, I I am proud that I am the wife of Arjun Shekhawat, and I will be proud of this for the rest of my life, even if I die, my husband's identity will be in front of him. Will give me peace, I have only given birth to you, but

I have not allowed you to get this soil, you have grown up playing in this, how can you get away from this soil As far as I am concerned, I am the wife of Arjun Shekhawat and this country is my first love and my last too. and if after all he is your dad, you think that I do not know that your dad is not a teacher, I knew this, yet I chose him because the lions of the jungle So only in the war they do their business, but your dad Jayshe humans rule the whole world, their place in their heart is different, whoever

Ordinary man cannot make it, he is not only immortal, God is that person in the world who rules the hearts of many people even after losing his life.

CHAPTER TWENTY-ONE

MISSION SAFFRON

It is said that there is a lot of motivation to do something in life, but I knew that day that the motivator is the condition of our house. If something is made, then why listen to other's words, if something is made, then give motivation to the heart and make the mind a motivator, they will listen to everything. After that I need to decide something because after one month that too in 2005 I qualified CDS and joined army.

After 1.5 years when my training was completed, I did not go home because I had promised my mother that I will not come back like this, means I came after winning, it was not a victory for me that I have become a lieutenant, they become every year's people, well why say in such things Is there a reason behind this too? 2008 Karachi (Pakistan) Maqbool Khan Shafaq Haider, you all must be thinking that who is this, so let me tell you that he is capable Whom India wants, means if our soil asks for love, then for its sake we definitely fear, but it has made our India a lot of trouble for China. Innocent lives were lost, I am not going to tell about that day because when I got this mission, Major Sunil had told me that this He should give his life away, or take his life, but don't let it fall into anyone's hands, one thing was very clear in USD that I am not going to die now and neither going to get their hands.

CHAPTER TWENTY-TWO

13 AUGUST THE UNTOLD SOTRY

2008 (March 27)..

To complete this mission, a team of slaves was prepared, headed by Captain Shravan Josh, who had the same thing as Major Sir, had to say that he was very happy for this on my first mission, because they say that if a soldier has blood of enemies on his hands .

His training is not complete until the LEOPARD hit him, and I was ready to give Maqbool the grave. Well, the trouble was that this mission was secret, meaning we could not go straight and break it, otherwise Pakistan was already scared. goes, so We all knew what we had to do, had made all our preparations to ask him upstairs, but the last thing the captain said was to use To get him alive and take him to India, this mission seemed impossible to everyone at that time because we could have died in that, but that pit was taken to India.

How could they have taken away, well, there is a special thing in the soldiers of India that they can set fire even in water, so the death of Maqbool was certain, well We took at least five months to settle down, because if we had attacked as soon as we left, the government would have drowned at that time, and One thing is famous in our army that we never do ours from behind like a coward, thats why after five months and that too on 13 August ,his grave was already ready, by the way people used to call him a big businessman of Karachi, thats why I had to give something in that gift Captain said that Biryani is prepared today on the last day, then what was it, all the cadets understood, and met him for the first time in that time. So I am doing all the bullets, let him see, then Pakistan will continue to cry, but for the sake of orders in our India.

Time For Pay Blood

I knew what I had to do, I gave him an offer at that time that I will give you 70 crores, but I want this thing? Means I was talking about Karachi's chili tea and the name of that chili was Draganov.

Ready for Chicken cut is to be done, but there is some touch which can disturb, then the captain said that we will take care of those things, you just bring him to the fort, and after that we did it as we had told, and in the days of age that chicken was brought to India, but how the question is still there, after all this How did it happen? Means there is not much hope to bring him, then how did this thing become possible, which seemed impossible some time ago, what did I say? There is a specialty in our army that we know how to set fire to water. But the question is still that how did we take it to India, it is said that sacrifice in the army is like victory, thats why we never think about the sacrifices.

Conquest

No, but why am I talking about sacrifices? I had also said that film heroes and military heroes are never the same, they definitely die. But behind the scenes and we are in the heart of our India, Pakistan is well known to the public, Maqbool Khan is very important for that. He can lose him at that time and we cannot leave him, I had heard that a soldier alone can fight with the whole country, but on the day when his own when I saw this reality with my eyes, I started feeling proud that I am also a soldier, and the specialty of a soldier is that he can do anything for his country. Maybe, we all knew that we all cannot return, yet we chose this path, well why so many dreams when reality is a pride So, when I was taking him near the fort, then at that time the soldiers of Pakistan attacked, at that time it was very difficult to get him out.

Become A Soldier

There was something because of which all of us could get out and it was someone's Quran, if one of us stops and confuses them, then all of them together. We would have faced him together but if we all had faced him together then Maqbool could have been released from Khan, at that time I remembered one thing of Major Sir, I had told him that knowingly knowing the coming of the witness, he said those things just like that, that too jokingly, but I did not understand those things at that time.

had taken a serious stand, then what was there even if my military brother won, he was not ready to agree, but I was also stubborn, I told him that I I will wait, you all take it, even then they were not agreeing, Subedar Sanjay was saying that I am not going to leave you, today If we mix them in the soil, they will become right on their own, on that day one thing should be known that the feelings we have in the army brothers are just like diamond Absolutely rare, even after all I told them that soldiers, I also want to eat Biryani, so keep the child for me and if I don't come then my Make sure to tell ma that her son has now become a soldier, that day I had decided two things that no matter what happens today, I will not lose today, even if I Why should death not happen on this earth .

Printed by Libri Plureos GmbH in Hamburg,
Germany